PIRACY

PIRACY

A NOVELETTE IN THREE ACTS

J. T. GODDARD

To Steve
who always enjoyed a good story
COYS

Act 1

The three-masted carrack rocked gently at anchor, large rubber tires providing padding against the concrete wharf. She was a replica of the *Nao Victoria*, Magellan's flagship for his attempt to circumnavigate the globe.

The ship had fulfilled the mission, but Magellan had not, falling and dying during the Battle of Mactan, in the Philippines, in 1521. Ship and man had traversed the Atlantic and the Pacific together and pierced the narrow and turbulent passage that now bore his name, but only she had also crossed the Indian Ocean and rounded the Cape of Good Hope, before the long northerly slog back to Spain under the command of Captain Elcano.

Neither had ever been here, to the eastern shore of this small island in the Gulf of Saint Lawrence, but the lure of an untapped sponsorship market had proven irresistible.

The metal platform bridging the gap between ship and shore juddered as people walked across. It was a simple piece of engineering, perhaps twelve feet long and three feet wide, four thick galvanized sheets welded together and edged by a two-inch square iron bar. From this rose thirteen slim pickets, each three feet high, with a simple metal spar welded to the tops and providing a handrail.

As the guests approached, a young man in a white uniform saluted, checked the proffered invitations, and then gestured each person towards the platform. As they stepped onto the highly polished wooden planks of Iroko and pinewood that constituted the weather deck, another young man in a similar naval-styled uniform played a brief welcome on a tin whistle, then ushered them under the white canvas tarpaulin and out of the rain.

It was all very organized, thought Bernie Veinot, leaning against the weathered wall of an old fisherman's shack in a generally vain attempt to stay dry. He didn't mind his jacket getting wet, he'd been out to sea in far worse conditions than this, but he didn't want the papier-mâché parrot on his shoulder to disintegrate before it had served its purpose to entertain and distract. A few women disembarked from private vehicles and huddled under an umbrella while their husbands parked the car and then marched steadfastly back. Twice a car went straight to the parking zone and a young couple ran laughing towards the ship.

Bernie rolled another thin cigarette and smoked it quietly, watching as the majority of the guests dashed from their cabs to the platform. Most people were obviously planning on this being an alcohol-fueled evening, he thought. He'd been to these gala evenings before and benefitted from them. For most of the men, two rums and they'd be on their knees. For most of the women, Bernie grinned to himself, two rums and they'd be on their backs.

The rain came down steadily, mostly vertical but every now and then a gust of wind would send the drops sideways. The afternoon had darkened quickly and the security lights on the wharf shone blurrily through the mist. Puddles were forming in the depressions left by heavily loaded trucks come to transport the catch back to the processing plants. Herring, lobster, haddock, crab, halibut; Bernie had fished them all, in season and out. He'd even gone out for tuna a couple of times, but that hadn't gone well. The north shore boys hadn't taken kindly to someone from the south-eastern tip muscling in on what they perceived as their own private goldmine, and a couple of intimidating near-misses had sent him scurrying back to his home port.

The flow of vehicles had slowed almost to a standstill. One or two taxis were still in the line to drop off their passengers, but no more cars were heading to the parking zone. He'd just about given up on her when he sensed the vibration from the phone in his pocket. He left the shelter of the shed and walked towards the man in uniform. He reached him just as the taxi door opened and Lisa Huckleberry got out, laughing at something the driver had said. She swirled towards Bernie and opened her arms for a hug and a kiss, then swerved away to hand their invitations to the sailor. Bernie wasn't sure whether the man was distracted by the cleavage or the parrot, but he waved them through with only a cursory glance at the printed cards.

He paused to let her cross the gangplank ahead of him. This provided the man with the whistle of a view not seen for many years, a replica image of Anne Bonney the Pirate Queen marching towards him. She was tall and statuesque, her bright red hair, testament to her Irish ancestry, falling in waves around her shoulders. Her yellow jacket clashed with her hair, as did her bright green pantaloons. A short sharp Cuttoe sword hung from her waist, suspended by a hook through the handguard, and she wore a flintlock pistol strapped to the other hip. While the young man nearly choked on his tin whistle, Bernie smiled to himself and admired the rear view.

The young man, having gallantly assisted Lisa through

the door, which was really simply a flap in the canvas wall of the tent covering the weather deck, gave hardly a second glance to the Long John Silver who followed her. Leaning lightly on his wooden crutch, a cutlass and a three-barrelled revolving flintlock pistol strapped to his waist, a tri-cornered hat on his head and a parrot on his shoulder, Bernie shouldered his way through the flap and entered onto the weather deck, so-called because normally it would be open to the elements. Now, however, it was protected by the canvas canopy, from which replica storm lanterns with electric bulbs swayed hypnotically.

It was not a big space, but it looked impressive. A small stage had been constructed at one end, towards the bow, on a half-deck that Bernie considered the fo'c'sle, and three musicians were playing a medley of shanties and other traditional songs. The singer had an acoustic guitar and was accompanied by fiddle and accordion. Their voices were comfortable enough on the ear but hardly audible over the chattering crowd, which reminded Bernie of a massed flock of crows gathering for their evening roost. He glanced around, trying to find Lisa, and saw the scarlet curls of her elaborate wig standing out above the heads of a group to his right.

Pushing through the press of people, he accepted a glass of 'grog' from a passing waiter and circled around so he approached Lisa from the front. She was surrounded by a group of older men, mostly dressed in tuxedos but a few in suits, all trying to look as though they were paying attention to her words while simultaneous looking down her decolletage. She saw Bernie coming and let out a shriek of delight, throwing open her arms and simultaneously thrusting out her breasts, much to the delight of her admirers.

"John," she called. "You made it!"

He excused himself through the outer band of admirers and lifted her outstretched hand to his lips, kissing it gently.

"Anne," he said. "You look ravishing."

She coloured, prettily, and assumed a downcast look with her eyes.

"You're too kind," she said, turning to her circle. "Isn't he too kind?"

They all agreed that he was but, Bernie thought, they were so mesmerized by her breasts that they would have agreed the sky was purple, as long as she asked them nicely. Now, however, she giggled.

"I was just telling these other guests," Lisa said, "how silly I feel. I told you and our other friends that we had to dress up," she giggled. "I thought that's what they meant by 'formal dress gala'. Aren't I just a silly one?"

She smiled coquettishly and placed her hand on the arm of the oldest man, a spritely gentleman who Bernie knew was in his seventies and still ran his car dealership empire with an iron fist. He smiled back and moved in towards her, putting his hand lightly on her waist.

"You look just fine, my dear," he said. "Just fine."

Lisa nodded, her curls bouncing, her chest heaving.

"Thank you," she said. "At least you'll be able to find me and my friends, we're the ones dressed up as pirates!"

The men laughed dutifully.

"And a very winsome one, if I may say so," said the car salesman, edging his hand higher on her waist and extending his thumb to caress the bottom curve of her breast.

Lisa glanced across at Bernie, who first grinned but then stepped forward. Before he could say anything, however, another voice cut through the general hubbub.

"Ah, *there* you are, Jeremy, I've been looking everywhere for you."

The car salesman dropped his hand as though he had been burned and turned to face the lady approaching from the back of the room. The stern, thought Bernie, where the bar was located. The lady pushed through and took Jeremy by the arm. She was younger than he by a full twenty years, but that still meant she was twenty years older than Lisa, and it showed in her makeup and her tired eyes, and in the way her equally impressive bosom was well camouflaged with a stiff linen jacket.

Bernie reached forward and took his partner's hand again.

"Come on, Anne," he said, laughing, "you can chat with these good gentlemen later. Right now, let's go and find our table, and the rest of the gang."

He nodded amiably at the circle of men, some of whom acknowledged him but most of whom stepped forward to give the Pirate Queen a firm, chest-squeezing hug. She pressed back, laughing, and they went off happily to find their wives. Bernie gently pulled her through the crowd until they came to a small door, on the other side of which a flight of stairs led down to the main deck. A smart-looking middle-aged man in a suit stood guard at the door.

"Sorry, sir, ma'am," he said, stepping across to block them. "We haven't opened the dining room yet. Please enjoy your drinks up here under the canopy until we make the announcement. It'll be about another half hour."

Lisa nodded, smiling.

"My fault, I'm sorry," she said. "I'm starting to feel peckish. Are you a security guard?"

The man snorted.

"Well, me and a couple of mates from the Legion have been asked to keep an eye on things, yes," he said. "But we're hardly special forces, are we?"

Lisa laughed,

"Thank you for your service, anyway," she said, and turned away. The man stopped her.

"Are you guys the entertainment?" he said.

Bernie laughed.

"Nah," he said. "Anne Bonney here managed to misread the invitation, and thought it was a fancy dress party. We figured with it being a galleon and all, we'd come as pirates. There's supposed to be six of us, if our friends aren't so embarrassed, they decide not to come!"

The guard snorted.

"It's not a galleon, it's a carrack," he said. "They're quite different you know."

Fearing a lengthy exposition on the subject, Lisa pulled on Bernie's arm.

"Let's find the ladies room," she said.

The guard looked sad at not being able to share his knowledge of sixteenth century sailing vessels, on which he considered himself something of an expert, but he graciously pointed towards the side of the ship.

"Go out of the tent and around the corner to your right," he said. "The toilets are all there, on the quarterdeck."

"Thank you," said Bernie, and led Lisa away.

They returned from the washrooms and rejoined the crowd without incident. Bernie collected two glasses of 'grog' from a waiter, and passed one to Lisa, with a hissed warning that she was not to drink any more. She nodded, and together they wandered around the edge of the room, chatting to people who caught their eye and explaining, over and over again, the misunderstanding about the invitations.

"Never mind dear," said one older lady, patting Lisa on

the arm, her own collection of eleven silver bracelets jangling against each other. "We're all dressing up, really. I've not had these rings out in years."

She waggled her other hand, the large jewel-encrusted bands glittering in the light. Lisa leaned over.

"Is that a black opal?" she said. "It's gorgeous."

The woman nodded, pleased.

"I brought it back from Kalgoorlie, in Western Australia," she said. "This green one is an emerald, from Regal Ridge, in the Yukon."

Lisa shook her head.

"Wow, they're amazing. What's this bright blue one?"

"That's lapis lazuli, from Afghanistan. I bought it at the market in Bamiyan, back in the early seventies. Where the giant buddhas used to be? It was on the hippie trail, y'know, and cheaper than Chicken Street in Kabul. And this pendant? That's a star ruby I got from Burma, what they call Myanmar these days."

Bernie looked at her lined face, thin white hair, and bright piercing eyes. She wore what he considered to be an 'old lady' dress, made from material that looked a lot like the curtains he remembered from his grandmother's house.

"You must have been really young, to be on the hippie trail in the seventies," he said, smiling.

She looked at him coquettishly, her eyebrows raised, and her cheeks dimpled.

"You're too kind, good sir," she said, laughing. "Listen, you couldn't find me a chair, could you? I can't do all this standing anymore."

Bernie nodded and walked back to the retired serviceman on door duty, who nodded and shook his head at the same time.

"Sorry, mate, no chairs on the weather deck. But if you want to bring her here and go down early, I'll let you in."

Bernie made his way back through the press of increasingly raucous people, guided by Lisa's bright red hair standing out above the crowd. Together they escorted the old lady back to the commissionaire and then edged slowly down the stairs to the main deck, which had been transformed into a dining room worthy of the greatest ocean-going liners of all time. At the bottom of the stairs was an emergency doorway, the fire door itself pulled open, through which they passed to the dining room.

The walls and floorboards shone; each plank polished to perfection. Dotted around were two dozen round tables, each draped with a heavy white damask tablecloth crowned by a glass vase of sunflowers and a metal tripod displaying the table number. There were eight place settings at each table, the polished silver cutlery reflecting the lights from the mock storm lanterns that had also been installed on this lower deck. A large noticeboard on an easel contained a large-scale map of the seating arrangements.

"Look for Muriel Stanhope, please," said the old lady, and Lisa quickly located the name.

"Table 15," she announced, and they made their way through the tables to the correct place, where they found Muriel's name on one of the embossed name cards. The old woman sat down with a grateful sigh, then patted the chair next to her.

"Why don't you sit a minute, dear," she said to Lisa. "Unless you want to go and listen to the speeches, of course?"

Lisa glanced at Bernie, who nodded, so they both sat down. Muriel looked at them with sharp eyes.

"So, Anne Bonney and Long John Silver, eh? One real and one fiction. Interesting choices for your disguise."

"It's not a dis ..." started Lisa, but Bernie broke in.

"Tell us about the hippie trail," he said. "What was that like? Why did you go there?"

Muriel looked at him and shrugged.

"It was the sixties," she said, as if that explained everything. "I was born here, on the Island, and it was a much staider place back then. There was no excitement at all. I ran away from home as soon as I finished high school, took the Abegweit across the Strait, this was long before the bridge of course, then hitchhiked to New York. I played my guitar and sang some songs, and in sixty-nine I went to Woodstock."

Her eyes misted over as she spoke, and her voice started to crack.

"Are you going to drink that grog?" she demanded. Bernie shook his head and pushed over the glass. She took a large gulp.

"Thank you. Where was I?"

"Woodstock," said Lisa, grinning across at Bernie. "The pop festival?"

"Right. I was eighteen. I fell in love with another singer, or thought I did, and made a right nuisance of myself. A proper groupie, I was. She liked me too. She used to call me Harold, even wrote a song about me. I followed her all around, and the next year we ended up at the Isle of Wight festival. In England."

"Who was that?" said Bernie.

"Never you mind," said Muriel, coughing, then taking another gulp of the rum and water concoction. "Do you think they'll let me smoke in here?"

Bernie shook his head. "No, there was a sign, no smoking on the boat."

"Shame. Anyway, we're in England, me and my friend, and we had an argument, so I left and went to London. I got a job at Lady Jane, in Carnaby Street. Have you heard of it?"

Bernie and Lisa both shook their heads.

"It used to be proper famous," said Muriel, sniffing. "It was the first real boutique. We used to sell see-through blouses, but it was considered indecent to wear them, so the girls would undress, just their tops, and we had an artist in the shop who would paint bras on them, then the customer could walk out in her new blouse."

Lisa looked at her in astonishment.

"What, take your real bra off and get a fake one painted on instead?"

Muriel grinned.

"It was a wild time," she said. "There was a way around everything. Anyway, there I was, in my miniskirt and my crocheted beanie hat, with my beautiful Mondrian Gogo boots, and this bloke asked me to go with him to Nepal. 'Kathmandu for Christmas', he said. It sounded interesting, and London was expensive, so I quit my job and we left."

"How long had you known this guy?" asked Lisa.

"A couple of weeks," said Muriel. "He was from somewhere up north, Yorkshire I think, and had a brilliant accent. I liked his smile. And he was good, if you know what I mean."

She winked at Lisa, who roared with laughter. Bernie looked from one to the other, perplexed.

"His name was John," said Muriel. "Like you," she laughed, nodding at Bernie. "We went down to Earl's Court in London, where all the Australians hung out. They used to drive these old vans across Europe and sell them, and then British and American hippies would buy them and drive to India or wherever and sell them back to Australians coming to England. Some vans made six or seven trips before they conked out. We didn't buy a whole van, but we took a share with another couple, they were Swedish, and we travelled together. We got to Kathmandu alright, but John wanted to stay and go to an Ashram in India, and I didn't. So, I left him."

She took another gulp of the grog.

"Long story short, I met this Aussie down on Freak Street, and we decided to leave Nepal. We travelled overland to Dhaka and took a coastal freighter to Bangkok. We had a week there and then went down to Perth by a passenger ship. Then me and Bruce, my Australian friend, we had a proper falling out. I discovered that he'd put a couple of pounds of hash in my backpack, without me knowing, and I'd carried it all the way from Nepal. He'd rolled it into sausages and stuffed them into the frame of my pack. I was furious. I'd carried this across four or five borders, I could have gone to jail for ever if someone had found it. 'That's why I didn't tell you,' he said. 'You'd have been nervous.' Shoot, I just about killed him."

Lisa stared at her.

"What did you do?"

Muriel shrugged.

"I made him sell it, then give me sixty per cent of the money. It was good dope; he got a good price for it. Then I bought myself a ticket on the new train that was going across Australia, the Indian Pacific, and I went to Sydney in style. I had my own bunk and everything. I also had a couple more of those rubies, so I sold them and did okay."

Just then people started coming down the stairs into the dining room, chattering to themselves as they looked at the seating chart and pushing their way through the tables.

"We'd better go," said Lisa. "Thank you for telling us those stories, Muriel."

The old lady looked at here steadily.

"I know who Anne Bonney was," she said. "I hope that pistol is not loaded?"

Lisa shrugged and smiled.

"See you later," she said, then followed Bernie as he walked away.

The room had filled up quickly and it took some time for them to find their table, which was to the side of the room, in a corner near the door to the kitchen. Unlike the other tables, this one was only laid for six diners, and did not have the fancy name cards found at the other tables. A couple dressed as Captain 'Calico Jack' Rackham and Grace O'Malley stood to greet them, each shaking Bernie's hand and leaning forward to give Lisa a quick peck on the cheek.

"Where's Mary and Martin?" asked Lisa, looking around.

Calico Jack grunted.

"Mary decided to stay in the back for now," he said. "People saw her laying the table and she doesn't want to spook anybody just yet."

Lisa nodded.

"Smart woman," she said. "Another half hour and some of this crowd won't recognize themselves in a mirror."

Calico Jack chuckled.

"It's not the guests who she's worried about," he said. "It's the other workers, the cooks and servers. She's convinced some of them are security in disguise."

"I doubt it," said Lisa. "We heard they've only got three commissionaires from the Legion. Where's Gordon, I mean Martin?"

"He's coming over now," said Grace, nodding towards the main floor. They turned and saw a man dressed as an Elizabethan dandy, wearing a gold vest over a white linen shirt with long sleeves and ruffed cuffs. He had a ginger beard and wore baggy pants which were strapped just below the knee, then gold stockings and a pair of white leather shoes. A long silver sword hung from his waist and a flint-lock pistol was tucked into his belt on the other side. A large white ruff around his neck completed the ensemble.

"Was Martin Frobisher really a pirate?" said Calico Jack.

"Not officially," said Lisa. "But he used to plan the attacks by the privateers. So he sort of counts. And Gordon thought he looked cool."

"No real names," he said, cautioning Lisa with a look. She nodded contritely

The man they were talking about stopped at a table and chatted with one of the guests.

"That's that nice old lady, Miss Stanhope," said Lisa. "Wasn't she a hoot?"

Martin Frobisher shook hands with the old woman, who ran her hand up his arm. He smiled at something she said, then continued over to the table and greeted everyone.

Bernie leaned forward and spoke quietly.

"How was it with those two at the gangway," he said. "Did anyone have any problems there?"

"Nah," said Calico Jack. "I held the door open for a guy as he left the cab and picked his pocket. He gave me a twenty-dollar tip! Anyway, the fellow at the gate just waved him through when he explained he was an MLA and must have forgotten his invitation at home. Grace and I just waltzed in on his ticket."

"Mary and I used those mock-ups you gave us," said Martin Frobisher. "No problem."

"Perfect."

Bernie leaned back and surveyed the room. The average age of the crowd appeared to be 'approaching retirement', although there were a few younger women and an even fewer number of young men. Most of the men wore formal jackets with their white ties, and the women were swathed in chiffon and silk. Small groups coalesced and separated, and nobody took any notice of the five young pirates sitting by themselves.

The band finished their introductory set to desultory applause and left the stage as a younger looking forty-year-old wearing a blue tuxedo, crisp white shirt, and red bow tie, bounded onto the stage. He clapped his hands together without effect, so raised the microphone and cleared his throat, loudly. Most people stopped talking and turned to him, but not all. He coughed a second time, then spoke clearly.

"Your attention please, thank you."

The chatter died away and everyone was looking at him, so he continued.

"Welcome to this Fund-Raising Gala," he said, smiling. "Before we begin, I would like to acknowledge that we are on the traditional and unceded territories of the Mi'kmaq Nation, and we acknowledge their long and stable stewardship of the land. I would also like to thank our platinum, gold, silver, and bronze sponsors, both of this evening and of our work in general. You will find their names listed on the pamphlets which we left on your tables, together with the envelopes for any additional donations you would care to make this evening. Thank you all for your support."

There was a round of applause, which the emcee allowed to run for a few moments before signalling for quiet.

"We are here on this famous ship," he said, "for two reasons. First, to support the Baroque by the Bay Ensemble, our local orchestra. It is because of your generous support that we are able to continue to preform. And second, to celebrate the adventurous nature of the early explorers, including Magellan, for whom our Foundation is named. The Magellan Initiative, as you know, provides support for young men and women from this area who wish to explore the world and leave it a better place."

He looked slowly around the room, trying to catch everyone's eye.

"I'm sure I don't need to tell you how fulfilling it is to support a young person with the opportunity to go on one of our missions to the rain forest of Borneo and count tree species, so that we have a better idea of the biodiversity of the planet. To go to the central plains of east Africa and dig wells, so that young children there can have fresh water to drink. To go to the pristine beaches of South America and collect the tonnes of discarded single-use plastic waste that washes up from the ocean each day, the detritus of our just-in-time economy and self-centred lifestyles."

Bernie observed that people did not applaud quite so enthusiastically for the last one, even though to him it was only one that might actually make a difference. An enhanced knowledge of biodiversity in Borneo would really only help investors in the pharmaceutical industry, looking to invent the next best thing in natural health and wellness products. Digging wells only really benefited the well-diggers, whose artesian pumps drained the aquifers and caused the potential for longer term drought. And all three examples, he noted, took approximately three days of the ten-day mission, with the rest of the time taken up by exploring the beaches, cuisines, and other attractions of the local area.

Lisa leaned over and whispered in his ear, her perfume wafting slowly into his consciousness.

"Don't look so cynical," she said. "Parents pay a good amount for their kids to go on those missions, and the Foundation helps with some of the costs, to be sure."

Bernie huffed.

"Sure," he said. "After skimming eighty percent off the

top for administrative expenses. It's all a con, Lisa, just another scam."

She kissed his ear, lightly.

"Which is why we're here," she murmured.

The evening progressed to the background beat of an increasing cacophony as the pre-dinner drinks consumed on the weather deck were followed by the four bottles of complimentary wine left at each table. The emcee had finished his introductions and promised that the silent auction would continue until the end of dessert, so people should visit often to make sure their bids remained competitive. The keynote speaker would be along between the main course and dessert, and a live auction would conclude the evening, but in the interim they should enjoy the famous Rollo Bay Rockers. The band returned to the stage and were afforded the same lack of attention as before.

Some people started wandering around the long tables set up against one side of the room, looking at the wide selection of donated items. A piece of paper and a pen were in front of each, so that people could make a bid on whichever took their interest. As bids were surpassed, keen potential purchasers circled back and upped their offers even further. Others were already returning to the bar for reinforcements before the main course was served, delicately side-stepping chairs and outstretched human legs as they carefully navigated the room. Nobody paid much attention as Grace stepped out of the room with a full bottle of wine and returned moments later with an empty one to stand on the table. As the servers placed plates of roasted chicken, mashed potatoes, carrots and green beans on their table, she gaily poured most of the fourth bottle into the nearly empty glasses.

"Can you get us another one," slurred Martin to the server who Bernie had identified as the possible third commissionaire. The man looked at him distastefully.

"You've probably had enough, sir," he said. "But if you want more, you have to go and pay for it now."

"I've never paid for it in my life," said Martin.

Mary dug him in the ribs with her elbow, and he winced. She smiled sweetly at the server.

"We're all travelling by cab," she said. "But thank you for your concern."

He nodded, then walked away. Bernie saw him lift his hand to his mouth to block a cough, and also saw him whisper quietly into his shirt cuff. Bernie made a small note on his napkin, then leaned over and carefully poured his drink into the terracotta base of the potted palm tree which stood against the wall.

"Time for you ladies to go to the bathroom, I think," he said quietly. "Martin, why don't you stagger back to the bar, see if you can attract that server's attention as you go. Calico Jack can go to the stage and ask the band to play something with a bit of yo-ho-ho in it. I'll go and visit near those two who are standing by the door, make sure it's locked properly. Lisa, give us five minutes then come back in and take over."

She nodded.

"Five minutes it is," she said. "Come on ladies."

She stood up, Mary and Grace alongside her, then put her hand on Bernie's wrist. She tapped his hand with a long, manicured fingernail.

"Five minutes starts now," she said, and they walked away from the table.

Act 2

Bernie reached over and took a small sip from one of the glasses on the table, then carried the glass with him as he made his way across the room. He stopped a couple of times to chat at a table, laughingly describing his many attempts to affix the parrot to his shoulder, leaning on his crutch as he told the story. He had just reached the open doorway when he heard a murmur run through the room. Turning, he saw Lisa had climbed the four steps to join Calico Jack on the stage and was now standing chatting to the band. They conferred between themselves and then nodded, and the fiddle player started a hornpipe beat. The accordion joined in, and then the singer took the microphone.

"Yo ho ho and a bottle of rum," he sang, tapping his feet. Lisa started to dance on the stage and the crowd began to clap along to the beat. This started to get faster, much to everyone's amusement, and her pantaloons ballooned out as her feet flew across the stage. Bernie looked at the two men by the door, raising his eyebrows in amusement, and they smiled back at him. Suddenly there was a gasp, and everyone turned as Lisa stumbled, grabbing hold of the lead singer to stop herself falling. With her free hand she pulled her sword from its scabbard and waved it above her head, then pulled the hair of the singer so that his head bent backwards, and she could hold the sword to his throat.

Calico Jack moved to the front of the stage and looked out, twirling his blunderbuss pistols to dissuade any heroic attendees from acting on their impulses. Bernie dropped his wine glass and tugged at the main stem of his crutch, which fell away to reveal a shotgun that he neatly raised to waist height and pointed at the two men. Across the room, he could see that Martin, now miraculously sober, had the waiter in an armlock and held a knife to his throat.

"Lock the door," said Bernie, gesturing with the shotgun. The man nearest nodded, his arms raised to his sides, and pushed the emergency fire door closed. His colleague leaned across to click the deadbolt.

"Now walk slowly to the stage," said Bernie, "around the edge of the room."

"Please don't be alarmed," said Lisa, her voice clear as she leaned into the microphone. "If everyone does as they're told, nobody gets hurt." The cacophony of surprised voices died down to a soft background hum.

Bernie reached the stage and nodded, indicating to the two men that they should join the band. Lisa released the singer, and he staggered back into the group, clutching at his throat. Martin frogmarched the waiter up and pushed him across to join the other five, all of whom Bernie shepherded towards the back wall. He stood easily, cradling the shotgun, lazily turning it through an arc that covered all six frightened faces.

"Sit down," he said. "Backs to the wall, legs out straight, hands in your laps." They complied.

He nodded to Lisa, who turned back to the microphone.

"Ladies and gentlemen," she said, laughing. "And those of you who are other, we want to be inclusive. Welcome. This is not going to take long. My colleagues here, Mary and Grace, are going to walk around from table to table. They each have a bag. In those bags, please put your wallets, jewelry, loose change. I'm sure you've all seen the movies; you know the drill. In a moment I am going to come down and pick a table, and then choose one person from that table. I will ask them to strip naked. If I find anything of value on that person, I will cut off their hand, and the hand of their partner, who should have reminded them of the treasure they forgot to give up."

She waved the sword above her head and paced the edge of the stage, then suddenly jumped down and walked to one of the tables.

"I pick this table," she announced. Grace rushed over.

"I didn't finish that one yet," she said. "Just give them one more chance."

Lisa turned her back.

"Twenty seconds," she said, and started counting. She gave no indication that she could hear the rattle of rings and bracelets, or the thud of a wallet. As she reached 'one' she turned and slammed her sword down onto the table. The edge bit into the wood, the tip pointed towards a wide-eyed young woman in her early thirties.

"You," said Lisa. "Stand up and strip."

"I knew they were bad 'uns," said Muriel. "Smart, but crooked."

She sniffed, then held her glass out for a refill. The

scruffy plain clothes police officer who had given his name as Sergeant Preston complied, pouring another hefty shot of black rum into the glass. She shook her head when his partner, a slim black woman introduced as Constable Parsons, offered her some water but nodded in appreciation as the woman held out an ashtray towards her.

They were sitting at a makeshift table out in the car park. It was almost ten o'clock in the morning, and the interviews had started about an hour earlier. The first officers on the scene had arrived at six thirty, alerted by a lobster boat captain that there was still a carpark full of vehicles on the wharf next to the tall ship. They had gone down the stairs and opened the door to a scene of utter chaos, where two hundred people had been trapped together all night. There was a foetid smell to the room, one the officers initially thought was human waste but which they soon realized had a lingering sulphuric odor. They had been methodical in their approach, and it had taken time to secure the site. They had separated the crowd into two groups, guests and service staff, and had tried to make sure that the perpetrators truly had left. Then they had brought the most elderly guests out first, Muriel amongst them.

"What happened?" said Preston, scratching his nose.

"We were halfway through dinner when this couple jumped on stage and told us we were being robbed," Muriel said. "The woman took charge. She scared the life out of everybody. Made three people take off their clothes, strip down to their underwear. I tell you what, though. She wasn't used to holding a cutlass or a dagger."

The second officer raised her eyebrows.

"What do you mean?"

"Well, there's a certain way you have to hold something like that. I used to have a kukri and I was taught to keep the blade facing up and out, ready to parry as well as thrust. She just held it down by her side and then used a chopping motion when she hit it on the table."

Muriel sniffed. Officer Parsons looked at her older colleague, who gave a slight shake of his head. She continued.

"Thank you. We might come back to that. Okay, the couple are on stage. Then what?"

Muriel snorted.

"Then they came around from table to table, holding these big sacks, and we had to give them out wallets, jewelry, anything valuable."

Preston cleared his throat, loudly, looking longingly at Muriel's cigarette and rum.

"What did they look like?" he said.

Muriel shrugged.

"They were in disguise," she said. "I don't think they'll look the same anymore."

"Please," he said. "Just describe what you saw."

Muriel stubbed out her cigarette, took another drink, and then placed her glass on the table.

"Alright, then. The one who was on stage and controlling things, she was Anne Bonney, the Pirate Queen. She was a tall girl, nearly six feet I'd say. Large chest, very prominent, and long bright red hair, but it was probably a wig. She was wearing a shiny yellow jacket, and jade green pantaloons; looked like a traffic light. She carried a short sword and a flintlock pistol."

"They were armed with guns?"

"They carried guns," said Muriel. "But they didn't fire them. I think they were replicas. Where would you get a working flintlock pistol in this day and age?"

"The internet?" said Preston, shrugging his shoulders. "Who knows? Okay, that's one of the women. Who else was there?"

"The guy with a real gun was Long John Silver. He had on a blue jacket, an old naval-type one with gold braid on the shoulders and the cuffs. Gold buttons down the front, and a blue tricorn hat, with gold pipe along the brim. He had a pretend crutch under his armpit."

"Why do you say it was a pretend crutch?" said Parsons.

"Because he wasn't really one legged, he just hopped like he was. It was like one of those swordsticks, you know? The shotgun was hidden inside, he just popped off the armrest and there it was. He had a pistol as well, and a long cutlass."

"Are you sure it was a shotgun?"

"Positive. Twelve gauge, I think. Single shot. We used to have one at the farm, for vermin."

Preston nodded.

"How did they speak? What were their accents?"

Muriel shrugged.

"Just normal. Native-born Islanders, I'd say."

"Would you now? Interesting. What about the others?"

"I didn't really see the others up close, except one. She came and took my jewelry, all my rings. I heard someone call her Mary, so I think she was supposed to be Mary Read, who was Anne Bonney's friend. Perhaps lover. She used to dress as a man and call herself Mark."

Parsons stared at her.

"How do you know this stuff?"

Muriel laughed.

"I read books," she said, "and I travel. I was down in Jamaica and learned all about the pirates, the real pirates of the Caribbean. Did you know, they set up their own state down there, back in the day? And I used to dress as a man, once, when I was young."

The two officers exchanged glances.

"This Mary, what did she look like?" said Parsons, clearing her throat.

Muriel looked up at the sky, trying to picture the image, then back at the police officers.

"Shorter woman, maybe five three or five four. Light brown hair, page boy cut, probably another wig. Burgundy half-robe over tartan plaid culottes, those short-legged trousers like golfers' wear. Smaller bust but she had on a push-up bra, so her boobs looked bigger, and she spilled out of her robe a bit. I suppose it stopped the fellows from paying too much attention to her face."

"And you?"

"Oh, it stopped me looking at her face as well," said Muriel, cackling.

"Did she have any weapons?"

"Cutlass and pistol."

"Thank you."

"You're welcome."

Preston consulted his notebook again.

"You've given us three very good descriptions, Missus Stanhope," he said.

"Mizz."

"Ms. Stanhope, I apologize." He cleared his throat. "How many others were there?"

"I think three more. Two men and another woman. One of the men took over on the stage, directing things when Anne Bonney came round the tables. I think he was supposed to be Captain Rackham, you know, 'Calico Jack'. The other guy was dressed like an Elizabethan toff, he was all in gold and white, had a ruff around his neck and everything. He was carrying the bags from the floor out to the door. I only saw the third woman briefly, a slight little thing. I'm guessing she was supposed to be Grace O'Malley, that's the only other famous female pirate I can think of."

Parsons broke in.

"Ms. Stanhope, what happened after they took the money and the jewels?"

Muriel shook out another cigarette from her packet. Preston leaned over the table and lit it for her, using his own lighter.

"Nothing, really. We were all sitting there, except for the three who had no clothes on. They were still standing, like they'd been told. The Bonney woman went back on stage and told us to stay where we were. The Long John Silver guy with the shotgun was up there with her, still keeping guard over the band and the other hostages. The rest of the gang all went to the door and left, carrying the bags. Then she told us they were going to leave us, and we had to stay where we were until rescued. The two of them went to the door and closed it behind them."

"What happened then?"

"Everybody started shouting and crying, all talking at once. Someone rushed to the door and shouted that it had been locked. I think people were starting to panic, then the emcee fellow went up on stage and took over."

"Thank you, Ms. Stanhope," said Sergeant Preston. "I'm going to go and speak to someone else now. Please can you stay here and give your details to Constable Parsons, then she will organize you a lift home."

"Is there any more of that rum?" said Muriel.

Sergeant Jim Preston walked around the tables which had been set up on the edge of the wharf, between the gangplank and the parking lot. The rain had finished overnight, although there were still a few puddles. Officers and civilian employees were taking statements, listening to shivering couples describe what they had lost. He knew most of them would not be as clear and concise as Muriel Stanhope had been. She had been flagged by one of the interviewers as having a story worth telling, and Preston tapped that officer on the shoulder as he went past.

"Thank you," he said, looking at the man and nodding at the young woman to whom he was talking. The officer inclined his head in appreciation.

Preston walked past the police tape and stepped behind the mobile command centre that had been driven down from Charlottetown. It was really just a converted recreational vehicle, but MCC sounded a lot more official. He took out his cigarettes and lit one, then read over his notes. He still had many more questions than answers.

A uniformed police officer stepped behind the MCC and saluted Preston.

"Sir, we've got the guy who was in charge of the event ready for you."

Preston looked at his half-smoked cigarette.

"Thanks," he said. "I'll be there in a minute. Get him a cup of tea, would you? Oh, and get Parsons."

The officer nodded and disappeared. Preston inhaled slowly, wishing he had the nerve to drink black rum at ten in the morning. 'Maybe when I'm seventy-five', he thought.

"My name is Jonathon Wainscott," said the man in the blue tuxedo, holding his head in his hands. "I still can't believe this."

"Please can you tell me what happened," said Preston. "Start at the beginning."

Wainscott took a gulp of the tea which had been given to him by a civilian volunteer.

"I'm the Executive Director of the Baroque by the Bay

Ensemble. We put on recitals all across the Island and have even been down to Nova Scotia a few times. This is, was, our major fundraiser, for the Ensemble and also for our Magellan Initiative. We sold two hundred tickets at a hundred dollars each."

Preston did the math in his head.

"Twenty thousand dollars? That doesn't seem like a lot, not for all this."

He waved at the three-masted tall ship still sitting at the wharf.

"I mean, you had to pay for her, right? And food, drink, musicians ..."

Wainscott scoffed.

"Not the musicians, no. They were our own, people from the Ensemble. They moonlight as a country-folk band, playing east coast stuff, so they agreed to help out. But the rest, yes. And yes, those costs did take up most of the revenue. But that wasn't where the profit was."

Preston sat back and folded his hands over his stomach, peering at Wainscott.

"No? Where was it, then?"

Wainscott stared back.

"Do you know the history of the Ensemble, Sergeant?"

Preston confessed that he did not. Wainscott nodded.

"We were started after the war. The second war, nineteen forty-seven. At first it was just a way for returned veterans to come together and listen to some music. You know, a couple of violins and a cello, a bassoon, and a small harpsichord. We played in the old community hall down at Holstein Bay. We kind of mooched along for twenty-five years."

Preston tapped his pen against his front tooth.

"That's all very interesting, but ..."

"Please, let me finish."

"Sorry, go on."

"In the early seventies, things changed. Like a lot of rural places in Atlantic Canada, this area became attractive to Americans. Draft dodgers, mainly. Hippies and other long-hairs, looking for an alternative lifestyle. But for all their faults, they loved music. A lot of them got involved in the Ensemble, and some of them had big ideas. We started to play in community halls, schools, churches, wherever we could. But then some people started to say we were becoming elitist, and that music should be for the people."

Wainscott sniffed and took another drink of his tea.

"We were always for *the people*, I think, but there you go. We always used to have raffles and things like that, silent auctions, and there were lots of arguments that the same people always won, because they were the only ones who had a cheque book. I won't bore you with the details, but the end result was a decision that all our events would be cash only, on a 'pay what you can' basis. We've moved on a bit since then, of course, and our fund-raisers are a bit more sophisticated, but we still have a cash-only rule."

Wainscott was flushed and had a bead of sweat running down his nose. Preston looked at him, calmly.

"How sophisticated?" he said.

"We were expecting to raise over two hundred thousand dollars last night," said Wainscott, glumly.

Preston gaped.

"In cash?"

Wainscott nodded.

Preston looked across at Parsons, who shook her head in disbelief.

"Are you telling us that you think the Pirates stole two hundred thousand dollars last night? From this ship?"

Wainscott nodded, slowly.

"Probably more. There would have been people who

didn't buy anything, or who came second in the bidding, and we might not have seen their money. And I heard they took people's jewels and watches and other valuable stuff, right? Who knows how much that's worth."

Preston scratched the side of his ear and looked at him.

"What would the Baroque by the Bay Ensemble do with all that money?" he said.

Wainscott shrugged.

"We have an annual budget of just under five hundred thousand. In addition to this fund-raiser, we get donations, apply for grants, sell subscriptions, and so on."

"Half a million dollars? For a small orchestra out here in the back of nowhere?"

Wainscott huffed.

"We are well-known and greatly respected," he said. "People come to hear us from all over the country."

Preston raised his hands in an appeasing gesture.

"Sorry, I didn't mean to imply anything otherwise. It just seems like a lot of money. What do you spend it on?"

"The Magellan Initiative sends three or four students overseas each year. That costs between twenty and twenty-five grand, depending on where they're going. For the rest, there's rent for the hall, of course, and some online costs for domain names and things. We hire a part-time social media person, and I receive a salary. We've got twenty players, it costs money to travel and perform, and people always need better gear, so we're always upgrading our instruments."

"Twenty?"

"Yes. We limit it to that number because we just wouldn't have enough space otherwise. Five violins, three violas, two cellos, a stand-up double-bass, three oboes, three bassoons, a post-horn, a kettledrum and the harpsichord. The only way you can join is if someone who plays your instrument leaves or dies."

Wainscott had pride in his voice, Preston noted, and sat straighter in his chair as he explained the strengths of the Ensemble. When he had finished, Parsons leaned forward.

"Who would have known there would be so much cash here last night?" she said.

Wainscott looked at her. "Anybody who asked, I suppose," he said. "It was no secret. This is the way we've always done it."

"Did you have any security?" said Preston.

"Yes," sniffed Wainscott. "Not enough, obviously. We hired three commissionaires from the Legion, they were helping us with security. And then we had two ex-Navy fellows, they dressed up like sailors and helped collect tickets at the dock."

"Could you give us their names and contact details, please," said Parsons.

Wainscott nodded. "No problem," he said.

Preston scratched his nose, thinking, then nodded to himself.

"Right, then," he said. "That's the background. Now, tell us what you saw. What happened?"

Wainscott took a deep breath.

"It was all going well," he said. "I'd given my 'welcome and thank you, now please spend money' speech, and the drinks were flowing upstairs on the weather deck. Everybody went down to the main deck for dinner, and I was on the lower deck with the food people when we heard some commotion. I went back up and this big woman was on the stage, telling everyone to be quiet, and this guy with a gun was taking the commissionaires to the front. I turned to go back down to the kitchens, but a young woman stepped out in front of me and pointed a pistol at me. She told me to sit down at a table, so I did. She kind of just stood there until the big woman told them to collect the money, then she came to our table with her bag."

"What kind of bag?" said Parsons.

Wainscott shrugged. "A big blue one. Like a mailbag, I guess."

Parsons nodded. "Thank you, please continue."

"They made us empty our pockets and throw everything into the bag; wallets, purses, watches, rings, mobile phones, whatever. Every so often the big woman would pick a table and make someone strip down to their underwear, to prove they weren't hiding any necklaces or money belts or whatever. Then they told us to stay put, and they left."

"Stay put?"

"Yeah. Her actual words were, 'shelter in place'. So, we just sat there until the door closed. Then all hell broke loose."

Wainscott shook his head and drank some more tea.

"It was mad. People yelling and shouting, trying to shake the door open, crying. So, I went up on stage and tried to calm things down."

Parsons looked at him.

"And did that work?"

Wainscott shrugged.

"Sort of, eventually. I got everyone to sit down again, and we made sure nobody had been physically hurt. I told the three people who had been made to strip to get dressed, and then the commissionaires went to check the doors."

"Doors, plural?"

"Yes. There are two sets of stairs down from the weather deck, the main one which we used and a smaller one, on the other side. It goes up to the fo'c'sle. But that one was locked as well. It shouldn't have been, it was the fire escape route."

"Did you see anybody lock it?"

"No. That guy in the fancy gold vest and pants, the one

with the beard, he was standing over there at one point, but I didn't see him touch the door."

"Thank you. Go on."

"We were thinking of breaking down one of the doors, but we couldn't, they were really solid and tight. And there was this weird smell, like someone had set off a stink bomb or something at the top of the stairs. I didn't know what to do, so I told the caterers to finish serving the meal. Not many people still had an appetite, though."

Parsons leaned forward.

"We found broken glass at the top of each staircase, sir," she said. "The tech guys think they might be from broken jars which had been filled with chemicals. When they were mixed together they gave off this horrible smell."

Preston nodded.

"Another intrusive but not invasive intervention," he said, half to himself. "It's like they didn't really want anyone to get hurt."

Parsons leaned forward again. "Did nobody have a phone?"

Wainscott shook his head. "There was one of the chefs, he had his, but he couldn't get a signal. The rest of us had been made to dump ours in the bags."

"So, you calm people down, and feed them, then what?" said Preston.

"Then we waited. There were some toilets on that deck, thank goodness, and we could go down to the lower deck. That's where the crew sleep when the ship is actually sailing, so there were bunks. I told the older guests to go and get some sleep down there, and we brought up blankets for the ones who were still on the main deck. Then we just sat there. I might have dozed a bit, but basically, I just kept wandering around to make sure everyone was okay. Then your guys turned up."

Preston closed his notebook.

"Thank you," he said.

Sergeant Preston and Constable Parsons sat on a pair of canvas-backed chairs he had picked up from beside an empty interview table. He had carried them behind the Mobile Command Post, and she had followed him, holding two paper cups of coffee. Now they sat facing each other as she sipped her drink and he carefully placed his on the ground, then lit a cigarette.

"What do we know?" he said.

Parsons scoffed.

"We know that a bunch of pirates came to a gala and walked off with nearly a quarter of a million dollars," she said. "We know that nobody got hurt. That's about it."

Preston shook his head.

"Not true," he said. "We also know that they knew their way around boats, they were able to find and lock the emergency escape route. They got in so they must have had tickets, so they will be on the guest list somewhere. We should check everyone who is here off against the master list. Make a note of that."

"Sir."

"They've done their research on pirates, that's for sure. Once we have a suspect, we can start to do internet history traces and find out what they've been Googling. We just need to find them first."

He picked up his coffee and slurped a long drink.

"Have we found those two sailors yet, the ones who were taking the tickets?"

"Yes, sir. Uniformed tracked them down. They only stayed around until everybody was on board, then they got paid and went to the bar in town. There are about twenty witnesses who saw them there all evening, drinking."

"Paid in cash, I suppose?"

Parsons laughed.

"Yes, sir."

"Hmmph."

Preston took a long drag on his cigarette, then spoke through the smoke.

"We have one good lead," he said. "The boss woman, that Anne Bonney, everyone says she was tall and buxom, and had bright red hair."

Parsons laughed.

"The hair was probably a wig," she said, "and I don't think you can go around looking for tall buxom women to take in for questioning."

Preston grinned at her.

"That's a shame," he said. "Can't I claim probable cause?"

She shook her head, smiling.

"Well, then, what don't we have?" he said.

She looked at her notes.

"We don't have fingerprints, everybody touched everything. We don't have strange accents, only a couple spoke and they 'sounded normal'. It's a conundrum, boss."

Preston stubbed out his cigarette.

"We know the motive," he said. "Just shy of a quarter million in cash is a good incentive. We know the opportunity, a bunch of unsuspecting partygoers in a TRE. And we …"

"Sorry, sir. What's a TRE?"

Preston shrugged.

"Old military term," he said. "It means 'Target Rich Environment'. All those guests confined to a small area. And third, we know the means. They were able to blend in by standing out, if you see what I mean. Dressing up as pirates was a brilliant disguise, and half a dozen people said that the Bonney woman told them what an idiot she was, to misunderstand the invitation. It was a master stroke in deception."

Parsons looked at him.

"So, we have means, motive, and opportunity, but not a clue who did it?"

"Basically, yes," said Preston. "But it's like Leonard Cohen said, 'there's a crack in everything, that's how the light gets in'. We just have to find the crack."

ACT 3

L isa Huckleberry thumped the teapot down on the table and returned to the fridge to get the carton of milk.

"I don't understand why we can't spend a little bit," she said. "It's not as though the bills are marked or anything."

Bernie Veinot poured himself a mug of tea and stretched out his legs.

"I've told you already, we have to live the same way as before, just until things calm down. You know what people are like. If you start buying a different type of cereal, they will ask you if you won the lottery!"

Lisa poured milk into her own mug, then offered the carton to Bernie. He shook his head, then spooned in two large teaspoons of sugar.

"I'm just glad today's Sunday, so I didn't have to explain why we weren't out hauling traps this morning."

Lisa huffed.

"That's easy. You could just have told them you woke up feeling headachy, wasn't sure whether or not it was COVID. One extra day in the water won't hurt the lobster."

"Well, it wasn't a problem," he said. "And hopefully we'll go out tomorrow, same as always."

"Exactly."

They drank their tea in silence, the morning sun streaming in through the small kitchen window.

"When are they coming?" she asked.

"I told them ten," he said. "About an hour."

"An hour?"

She got up and came around the table to stand behind him, then leaned forward so the back of his head was nestled between her breasts.

"We didn't really celebrate when we got back last night," she said, moving her shoulders from side to side. He lifted his tea and took a sip, grinning.

"Didn't want to wake the kids," he said.

"They weren't here, silly," she laughed, "you were just too tired. Anyway, they're at mom's until teatime."

"That's true," he said, putting his mug back on the table and reaching his arms up above his head. He unzipped her fleece, delighted to find she wasn't wearing a bra. She moaned as he played with her nipples. Given a final squeeze, he let go and stood up, then turned around. She looked at him lustily, breathing deeply, and reached for his belt. He hooked his thumbs into the waistband of her yoga pants and pushed them down, then swung her round so her back was against the table.

"No time for bed," he said, his jeans around his ankles, and leaned over to move the tea pot as she lay back and spread her legs for him. She was always vocal when they made love and, when they had first met, he had worried that the neighbours would hear. She had made him watch the last scene of '*La grande séduction*' a few times and he had eventually lost most of his caution. Now, when she screamed the third time and squeezed her legs hard around his waist, he simply laughed and kissed her to muffle the sound.

Bernie stepped back and pulled up his jeans, watching as she lay quivering on the table, gasping in air as she slowly caught her breath. He ran his hand up her body and touched his fingers to her lips. She kissed the tips, softly.

"More tea?" he said, and she slapped his hand away, laughing, then caterpillared herself off the table.

"I'm going to get showered and changed," she said, "now that you've had your wicked way with me."

"It was your idea!" he protested.

She laughed, picked up her yoga pants, and walked out of the kitchen.

Gordon and Jenna arrived first, promptly at ten o'clock, and they both accepted a cup of tea. They had nearly finished when a loud engine signalled the arrival of Richie and Gloria. They walked into the kitchen and put their motorcycle helmets on the floor near the door. The men shook hands with each other and hugged the women, the women hugged each other and laughed.

"Sorry we're late," said Gloria. "I was in the shower."

Lisa giggled. "Me too!" she said.

Jenna shook her head. "I got mine last night," she said, winking.

Bernie looked at the other two men and shrugged. He brought over some more mugs and a fresh pot of tea, then they all sat around the table. Lisa reached out with a dishcloth and gently wiped a small area.

"You must have spilled a drop earlier," she said to Bernie, who flushed crimson and looked away. Lisa shook her head, her short blonde hair hardly moving.

"Well," she said, "we did it! Cheers!"

She lifted her mug and they all followed suit, toasting each other in turn.

There was a silence, then Jenna cleared her throat.

"Umm, where are the bags?" she said.

Bernie had paled back to his normal colouring, so he glanced at her and nodded.

"In the shed," he said. "We'll get them in a minute. First, we need to go over the ground rules again."

Richie chuffed.

"We've done this a hundred times," he said.

"Humour me," said Bernie.

Gordon shook his head.

"Okay," he said. "Let's get it over with. We split the cash equally, three shares. We divvy up the other stuff and each of us is responsible for getting rid of it for as much as we can. In a month we'll meet again to share that money, and to decide what to do with anything that's left."

"You forgot something," said Bernie.

Gordon looked at him. "What?"

"We split the cash equally, but ..."

"... we don't spend any of it," finished Jenna.

Lisa huffed.

"I think that's silly," she said.

"It's what we agreed," said Bernie, and Jenna nodded.

"Yes," she said. "We have to be absolutely normal for the next two weeks. Then we can go to Halifax and have some fun."

"We should be able to take a little bit," said Gloria. "Like, a hundred bucks each or something. Just for fun. Nobody will notice if we've got a little bit of spending money. We can just say they gave the boys a bonus, as a thank you for all their hard work this season."

"Season ain't over," said Richie. "Although it would be nice to be able to fix that muffler."

"A hundred bucks ain't even a bag of groceries these days," said Gordon. "I don't reckon anyone would notice."

Lisa smiled at Bernie.

"Looks like you're outvoted, four to two," she said.

He scowled, folding his arms.

"Don't pout," she said. "Go on, go and get the bags."

Bernie stood up and walked out of the kitchen, followed by Richie and Gordon. The three women smiled at each other.

"I don't know about you two," said Lisa, "but I got a proper pounding this morning. It was good for us to release all that tension that's been building these past few weeks. More tea?"

Jenna and Gloria giggled, holding out their mugs, and then the three chatted quietly until the men returned.

It took them three trips. There were seven bags, each a large canvas sack. Five had once held fifty kilos of soybean meal and two were old post-office delivery bags. Once all the bags were in the kitchen, Bernie and Richie lifted the first onto the table. They upended it carefully and watched in awe as the banknotes all spilled out.

"Let's sort them first," said Lisa. "Then we can count."

"I'll do the hundreds," said Jenna.

"Fifties," said Gloria.

"Bernie and I will do twenties, there's more of them," said Lisa.

"I'll do tens and you can do the fives," said Gordon, looking at Richie. "That okay?"

Richie nodded and leaned forward to start pulling the blue notes from the pile.

∼

At noon they stopped for a break. They had soon realized that there was not enough room on the table and so Bernie had gone to his basement and come back up with half a dozen cardboard boxes.

"I got 'em from the liquor store," he said. "We were trying to sort out the garage last winter."

Carefully, the piles of sorted banknotes were moved to the boxes, and the sorting continued. When they paused, they had emptied three bags and were about to start on the fourth.

"One more after this," said Bernie. "The last two are both full of jewelry."

Lisa looked at the clock on the stove.

"The kids will be back soon," she said. "Maybe we should just finish the cash and leave the other bags until tomorrow?"

The others nodded, but Jenna coughed.

"No offence, Lisa," she said, "but if we're leaving all this cash here tonight, can we seal the boxes?

"What. Don't you trust us?"

Lisa raised her voice angrily. Jenna tried to appease her.

"It's not that, it's just ..."

"It would just make us more comfortable," said Gordon. "Then there's no hint of wrongdoing, y'know?"

Ritchie and Gloria expressed their agreement. Bernie looked up from the table.

"It won't hurt," he said. "I've got some duct tape; we can seal the boxes and then sign across the tape. That way we know that everything's okay."

"I still think we should trust each other," Lisa huffed, "but if you insist."

She left the table and dug around in a kitchen drawer, returning with a pair of scissors and a thick tipped felt pen. She put those in front of Bernie.

"Here you go," she said, and returned to counting the twenty-dollar bills.

At three o'clock they called it quits. Lisa made another pot of tea and placed a plate of chocolate chip cookies on the table.

"I made these the other day," she said. "Help yourselves."

Bernie taped the liquor store boxes closed, and everyone took the pen and initialled across the tape, making sure their signature went out onto the cardboard as well.

"We'll count these out later," said Bernie. "Monday tomorrow. I'm going to have to call in sick to the boat, what about you lads?"

Ritchie nodded. "I'll be here," he said.

"Me too," mumbled Gordon, his mouth full of cookie.

Bernie looked across at Lisa.

"What are the kids doing tomorrow, d'ya know?" he said.

She shrugged. "Normal day," she said. "On the bus at eight, back at four."

"What's a good time for youse guys?" said Bernie. "After eight, like?"

"I'm on evenings this week," said Gloria, who worked the check-out at a local store. "Anytime's good."

She didn't articulate what they all knew; that Richie had recently been fired from his job as a mechanic and was currently unemployed.

Gordon looked at Jenna, who rolled her shoulders.

"I'll call in sick tomorrow morning," she said. "The school will just bring in a substitute EA to help with Donny."

Bernie nodded, then checked across to Gordon.

"What about you, Gordie?"

"I'm good. I'll just tell Catherine that something came up. She won't care, harvest is only just starting so we're not getting many potatoes to the warehouse, not yet. I'll do an extra shift one evening if she needs more stock moved into storage."

"We're all good, then," said Bernie.

Lisa scoffed.

"Don't mind me," she said. "I'm just a stay-at-home mom. My life doesn't count."

Bernie went red, this time from embarrassment.

"No, I didn't mean that," he said. "Sorry, Lisa. What is your day like tomorrow?"

"Well," she said, "thank you for asking. I'll get the kids on the bus, clean up the disaster area that you guys always leave in the kitchen, then go and paint my nails before sitting down to watch Kelly and Ryan. I'll check Facebook and maybe do some online shopping, have a quick visit from my fancy-man during his lunchbreak, and then go for a long bath. Then I'll make your supper so it's ready when you get home."

Jenna giggled.

"You asked for that," she said.

Bernie nodded, ruefully.

"Okay, Lisa," he said. "Will you be able to spare us some time during your busy day?"

She shrugged.

"I can record the tv," she said. "Facebook and shopping will wait. And if we're running late, I'll text Gérard and tell him not to come."

Gloria raised her eyebrows.

"Gérard?" she said.

"Depardieu," said Bernie, shaking his head. "Gérard Depardieu; he's her fantasy lover."

"Do you have to wear a big nose and a floppy hat?" said Gordon, and they all laughed.

"Only if we're back in early from hauling traps," said Bernie, joining in. "Why do you think I hang around the wharf after we've unloaded?"

Jenna snorted and coughed, and Richie slapped her on the back. His hand rubbed between her shoulder blades and then up past her shoulder to caress her neck. 'Interesting', thought Lisa, but didn't say anything. She clapped her hands together.

"Let's focus, people," she said. "Eight-thirty tomorrow morning, here?"

Everybody agreed, and shortly afterwards the other two couples left. Bernie carried the mugs to the sink and washed them while Lisa put the cookies away and then picked up a dish towel.

"What's a normal shift for Gordon," she asked.

"At the warehouse? Depends on the time, but they store twenty million pounds of potatoes in there, so he's driving that tractor pretty hard all day. He's not home much before eight on a normal day. Why?"

"Just wondering. Ritchie seemed to be a bit friendly with Jenna."

Bernie looked at her. "And ...?"

"Well, I was just thinking, that's all. Gordon's at work until late, Gloria is doing afternoon shifts, Jenna finishes at three when school lets out, and Ritchie is unemployed with no commitments."

"Lisa, that is absolutely nothing to do with us," he said. "Don't even think that stuff."

"It might be something to do with us when we all have money," she said.

A brisk north-east wind set up during the night and brought with it cooler temperatures, rain, and blustery winds. Bernie lit the woodstove for the first time that fall, and the kitchen was warm and cosy when the other four arrived just before nine. This time he paid more attention to the interactions between Ritchie and Jenna, noting the fractionally too long hug and the brushing of hands as they passed each other. Gloria and Gordon, it seemed, were oblivious to what was happening.

As soon as her kids had gone to school, Lisa had helped Bernie to bring the sealed boxes up from the basement and these were arrayed on the table. She brought out a small paring knife and stood poised to open the first box.

"How shall we do this?" she said.

They all looked at each other. Gloria cleared her throat and looked around, diffidently.

"When we're cashing up," she said, "we count the notes first, by denomination. Then we add up all the totals. We could do that."

"Sounds good," said Jenna, and the others nodded. Lisa took the knife and pulled a box towards her.

"We'll start with the fives, then," she said, and slit open the tape.

They took a coffee and bathroom break at ten, and at noon drove into town for lunch at one of the coffee shops. It was busy, but Lisa found and commandeered a table while the others waited in line to order. They ate their sandwiches and treated themselves to crullers for dessert, then returned to the house and continued to count. At two-thirty they sat around the table, staring at each other and at the tabulated row of figures on the calculator print-out.

"Holy shit," said Ritchie, leaning back. "Are you sure that's right?"

"I've done it three times," sniffed Gloria, "and Jenna added them up as well. Yes, it's right."

"Two hundred and forty thousand dollars," said Bernie, quietly shaking his head. "That's eighty thousand each."

"And we still have the jewels, watches, and stuff," said Lisa.

"I counted the coins," said Jenna. "It was mostly loonies and toonies, but some people did have quarters. There was another four hundred there. I think we should just give that to the donation box at the school."

"Or the one at church," said Gordon.

"Maybe half and half," said Lisa, nodding. "That's a detail. Let me go and get the jewelry."

She left the table and returned with one of the old soybean sacks, which she emptied onto the table. The watches, necklaces and rings clattered out, forming a small pile which Jenna gently smoothed out with her hand.

"They're gorgeous," she murmured, poking her finger through the pile. "Look at this one!"

She lifted up a thin silver necklace, from which hung a round dark-red gemstone cradled in a filigree basket. As the light caught the surface, six bright rays pointed out from the centre.

"That's a star ruby," said Lisa, authoritatively. "From Myanmar. What used to be called Burma."

Jenna stared at her.

"How do you know that?"

"Because I told her," said a voice from the doorway.

The group turned as one, like spectators at a tennis match, and stared at the small figure in the doorway. She smiled back.

"May I come in?" she said.

Lisa nodded, stepping forward robotically and bringing an extra chair to the table. The woman came forward and sat down.

"Thank you, dear," she said. "Allow me to introduce myself. Muriel Stanhope is the name I gave to the police, and that is good enough for now. Who are you?"

Lisa looked at the others, then back at the woman.

"I'm Lisa," she said. "Do we need last names?"

The woman shrugged.

"I don't care," she said.

Bernie coughed and introduced himself. Muriel nodded.

"I remember you two," she said. "Long John Silver and Anne Bonney. And what are the real names for Martin Frobisher here, or Captain 'Calico Jack' Rackham? Hmmm? Not to mention Mary Read and Grace O'Malley?"

"I'm Gordon," said Gordon. "I was Frobisher. This is Jenna, she was Mary. That big biker over there, he's Ritchie, he was Calico Jack. And this is Gloria, who was Grace O'Malley."

"You forgot the scar on the face," said Muriel. "From where the eagle attacked her."

They all just looked at her. Bernie was the first to break the silence.

"What do you want?" he said.

She laughed.

"Oh, not a lot," she said. "I'd like my personal jewels back, please, and an equal share of the cash, to make up for all the trouble you've put me through."

Bernie huffed.

"An equal share?"

"Yes," she said. "I'm figuring you're three couples, correct?" They nodded affirmatively. "Well then, it's easy. Instead of three equal shares, we'll make it four. Let me see ..."

She picked up the paper from the calculator and glanced at the total, then smiled.

"Easy-peasy," she said. "Sixty thousand a share, instead of eighty. All nice and clean. I'd like a mixture of notes, please, dear."

This last comment was directed to Lisa, who reached into the nearest recycled wine box and silently pulled out a handful of notes.

"Hang on," said Ritchie, standing up and moving aggressively forward. "Why are you paying her? Why don't we just bang her on the head and throw her into the ocean?"

Muriel tilted her head to one side and looked at him.

"Because you're not stupid," she said, "and you're not killers. And also, because I went to my lawyer's office earlier and have left full details of where I am this afternoon. I'm not out to steal from you. I just want my share; and my jewelry back."

Bernie coughed.

"Sorry," he said. "Excuse me, but why do you deserve a share?"

Muriel shrugged.

"Because I'm here without a policeman," she said. "But don't underestimate them. I figured it out, and I'm sure they will as well, eventually. So, you'd better get rid of the evidence, hide it away somewhere safe."

Bernie nodded.

"How did you figure it out?" he said.

Muriel smiled.

"I'm just an old lady," she said, "so people expect me to do 'good works'. I volunteer at the library. You were all too perfect. You had obviously done a lot of research. That gave me an idea. The famous pirates like Long John Silver and Calico Jack Rackham are easy, but there's only one book that really describes people like Anne Bonney and Mary Read. This morning I went in and volunteered an extra shift. I logged on to find out if anyone had borrowed Johnson's book, *A general history of the pyrates*. And guess what, they had!"

She looked around, mischievously.

"Not only that, I found that the same person had borrowed Klausmann's book on women pirates as well, and the Sanders one about Bartholomew Roberts. So, I did something naughty, something we're not supposed to do. I looked up your real name and address. Lisa Huckleberry. That's a lovely name. And here I am."

She gestured with her arms, palm out, as though this was a magic trick.

"Come on," she said, "or my share will increase. You two, count out sixty thousand for me please, mixed notes."

This command was directed at Jenna and Gloria, who looked to Bernie for advice. He nodded, ignoring the angry mutterings coming from Ritchie. Gordon simply sat there, smiling to himself at the absurdity of it all. Muriel turned to Lisa and Bernie.

"You two know what my rings look like," she said. "Come on, let's find them. I'll take the pendant first, dear."

She reached across and took the star ruby from Jenna's hand, the contact startling Jenna into action. She looked at Gloria, then took the handful of notes from Lisa and started counting. Muriel pointed into the scattered collection of jewelry.

"There's the lapis lazuli," she said. "Now, where are the black opal and the emerald?"

When she had left, the six of them sat around the table in shocked silence. She had produced eight large rubber bands from her purse and used those to loop the notes into manageable amounts. She had carefully placed the rings and pendant into a small velvet jewellery bag and then put that in the purse as well. She had poo-poohed the idea of taking more jewels.

"That's how they'll catch you," she had said. "You'll have to take them to a pawnshop or a fence somewhere off Island. But even then, someone will blab. No, the cash is enough for me, thank you."

Bernie had taken a deep breath and asked the question that had been troubling him since the beginning.

"Is your name really Muriel Stanhope?" he said.

She smiled.

"That's for me to know and you to think about," she had replied. "It has been a useful name. Not one you might find at the library, though, should you go looking."

Bernie bit back a laugh.

"I wouldn't dream of it," he had said.

Now they looked at each other.

"The kids will be home soon," said Lisa. "We'd better get this cleared away."

Gordon cleared his throat.

"I think I'll just take my share and be going," he said. "I agree with Muriel, the jewels are not worth the hassle."

"Your share?" said Jenna. "Don't you mean our share?"

"Nah, you're right," said Gordon, smiling sadly. "You take your half and work things out with Ritchie. And Gloria, I guess. I want nothing to do with it. I'm outta here."

Gloria paled and looked towards Ritchie, who had

turned bright red. Then she looked at Jenna, who couldn't meet her eyes.

"What's going on?" she said, her voice breaking.

Gordon got up and shook hands with Bernie, then gave Lisa a hug.

"Thanks for everything, guys," he said. "I'm taking my share and going off Island. The potato industry can manage without me this year."

"It's for the best," he said, looking at Jenna, who had started to cry. "I'll get in touch about the house and stuff."

He nodded at Ritchie, placed his hand gently on Gloria's shoulder, then walked out of the door and into the summer afternoon. They heard the car start, then the sound of the engine slowly faded away.

Sergeant Preston folded his arms and leaned back against the concrete wall of the parking lot. He glared at Constable Parsons.

"Where's the crack, then?" he said. "Why can't we see anything?"

She shook her head.

"I don't know, sir. It's like they've all just disappeared."

He huffed, then took out another cigarette and lit it. He spoke around the exhalation of smoke.

"That woman who knew all about pirates, where's she gone?"

"Ms. Muriel Stanhope," said Parsons, reading from her notes. "She was the one who drank all that rum as well."

Preston nodded, grumpily.

"Yes. To 'calm her nerves', she said. I'm starting to think she was ice cold and just took us for a ride."

"Well, she's not at that address she gave us, sir. In fact,

nobody is. There isn't a house. It's just an empty lot in a new development up on the North Shore."

"What was the address again?"

"Mountebank House, sir. She said it was a home for 'retired ladies' on Cassie Chadwick Drive. But uniform went up there and it's just a big field with a civic number."

"Hang on a minute," said Preston, stubbing out his cigarette and pulling his phone out of his pocket. 'Cassie Chadwick', you say?"

"Yes, sir."

His thumbs moved rapidly across the screen, typing the letters into a search engine. He pressed send, then waited. A moment later, he smiled sadly to himself, and looked across at Parsons.

"We have been well and truly conned," he said.

"What do you mean, sir?"

"I should have seen it earlier. 'Mountebank' is a fraudster, a conman. And now, this."

He waved his phone at her.

"Cassie Chadwick. 'The most well-known pseudonym used by Canadian con artist Elizabeth Bigley, who defrauded several American banks out of millions of dollars.' Shit shit shit."

Parsons looked at him.

"Do you think she was in it with them?" she asked.

Preston shook his head.

"I don't see how," he said. "She lost all that jewelry herself, others at the table corroborated that. But who knows? Stranger things have happened."

The two officers looked at each other. After a long pause, Parsons spoke again.

"When are you officially retiring, sir," she said.

"On Friday," he said. "We've got three days to solve this so I can wrap up the paperwork."

Parsons shook her head.

"It's not going to happen, boss," she said. "Sorry, sir."

Preston grunted.

"I know," he said. "We have absolutely nothing, just a bunch of rich people who lost money and insured jewelry that was probably highly over-valued. This one won't stay as a high priority case for long. They'll probably let you keep poking away for a couple of weeks, and then it will go into the cold case drawer, and you can get on with more exciting things."

She looked at him.

"So, what should we do next, sir?"

He snorted.

"Let's go and have a drink," he said. "The sun must be over the yardarm somewhere."

Gordon drove his car steadily along the road that wound around the southern shore of the river, one of the three which gave the area its name. He dropped down into the local town, past the traffic lights at the gas station and then over the bridge with the large metal sculptures of cormorants standing on posts. As always, he smiled at the two competing craft breweries that faced each other across the marina. He pulled into the large parking lot that served the bank at which he and Jenna had their accounts. His card would only allow him to take out a thousand dollars a day, so he withdrew that, then drove further up the hill to the Tim Hortons.

He went into the washroom and changed from his tee-short to the Martin Frobisher shirt, hoping that the arms of his jacket would cover the ruffed cuffs. He tossed the tee-shirt into the waste basket and went back into the main building, buying a medium double double to go and an apple fritter. Then he returned to his car and drove out of town, following the highway through the lush countryside. He saw the large tractors plowing the land, the conveyor belts moving the potatoes into the closely following trucks, the trucks themselves pulling onto the highway and leaving broad streaks of bright red mud to mark their passing.

At the hamburger restaurant on the causeway, he pulled into the parking area and sat for a moment, thinking. Then he got out of the car and walked over to the bins by the door, depositing his coffee cup and the wrapper from the fritter. The door opened and she came out, holding two of the famous burgers in one hand and pulling a small roll-on travel case with the other.

"I thought we could eat in the car," she said. "I'll be more comfortable once we're over the bridge and on the mainland."

Gordon nodded, opening the passenger side door for her. He took her case and put it in the back of the car, next to his small bag, then climbed into the driver's seat and took the proffered hamburger. She ran his arm up her sleeve.

"I do love a man in linen," said Muriel Stanhope.

About the Author

J. T. Goddard is a retired educator. Born and raised in Yorkshire, his career took him to every province and territory in Canada, and to many countries around the world. He now happily calls Prince Edward Island home. He has written three mystery novels, *Traces, Tracks*, and *Missing*.

Find out more at: www.jtgoddard.com.